D1310826

DATE DUE

My 1ST GRAPHIC NOVEL

BREE'S BIKE JUMP

My First Graphic Novels are published by Stone Arch Books
151 Good Counsel Drive, P.O. Box 669
Mankato, Minnesota 56002
www.stonearchbooks.com

Library of Congress Cataloging-in-Publication Data
Mortensen, Lori, 1955-
Bree's bike jump / by Lori Mortensen ; illustrated by Mary Sullivan.
p. cm. — (My first graphic novel)
ISBN 978-1-4342-1620-5 (library binding)
1. Graphic novels. [1. Graphic novels. 2. Bicycles and bicycling—Fiction. 3. Fear—Fiction.] I. Sullivan, Mary, 1958- ill. II. Title.
PZ7.7.M67Br 2010
741.5'973—dc22

2008053377

Summary: Bree wants to go off the big bike jump at the field, but she is too scared. Find out if Bree can face her fears.

Creative Director: Heather Kindseth
Graphic Designer: Carla Zetina-Yglesias

Printed in the United States of America

MY 1ST GRAPHIC NOVEL

BREE'S BIKE JUMP

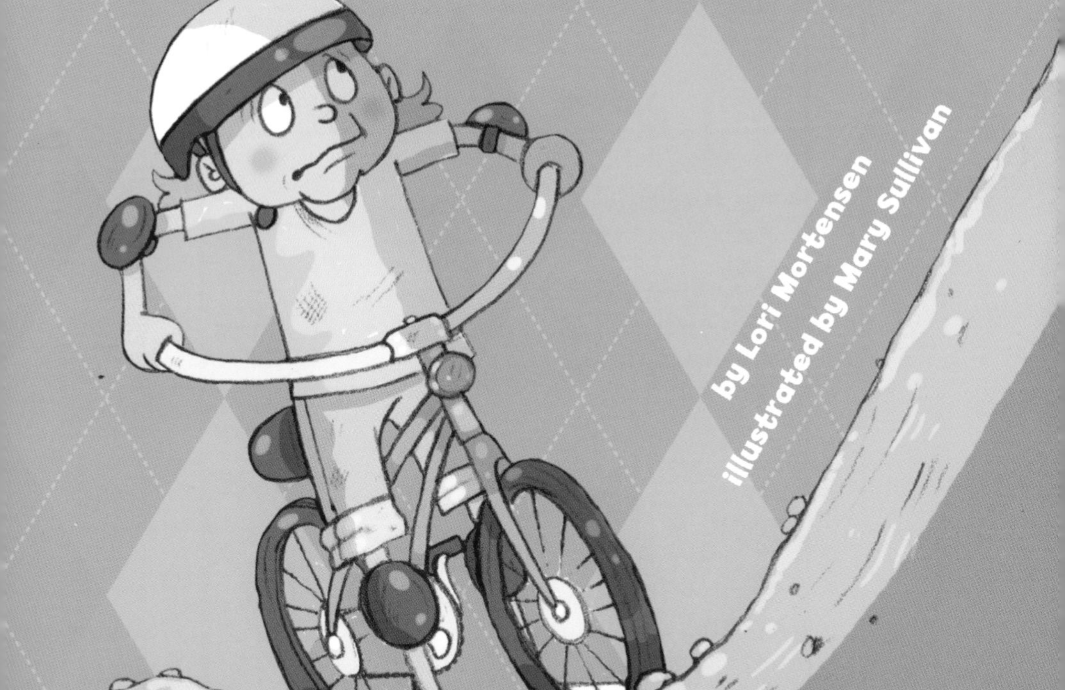

by Lori Mortensen
illustrated by Mary Sullivan

STONE ARCH BOOKS
MINNEAPOLIS SAN DIEGO

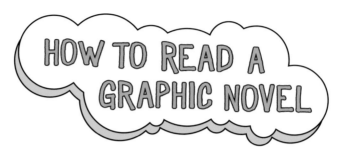

HOW TO READ A GRAPHIC NOVEL

Graphic novels are easy to read. Boxes called panels show you how to follow the story. Look at the panels from left to right and top to bottom.

Read the word boxes and word balloons from left to right as well. Don't forget the sound and action words in the pictures.

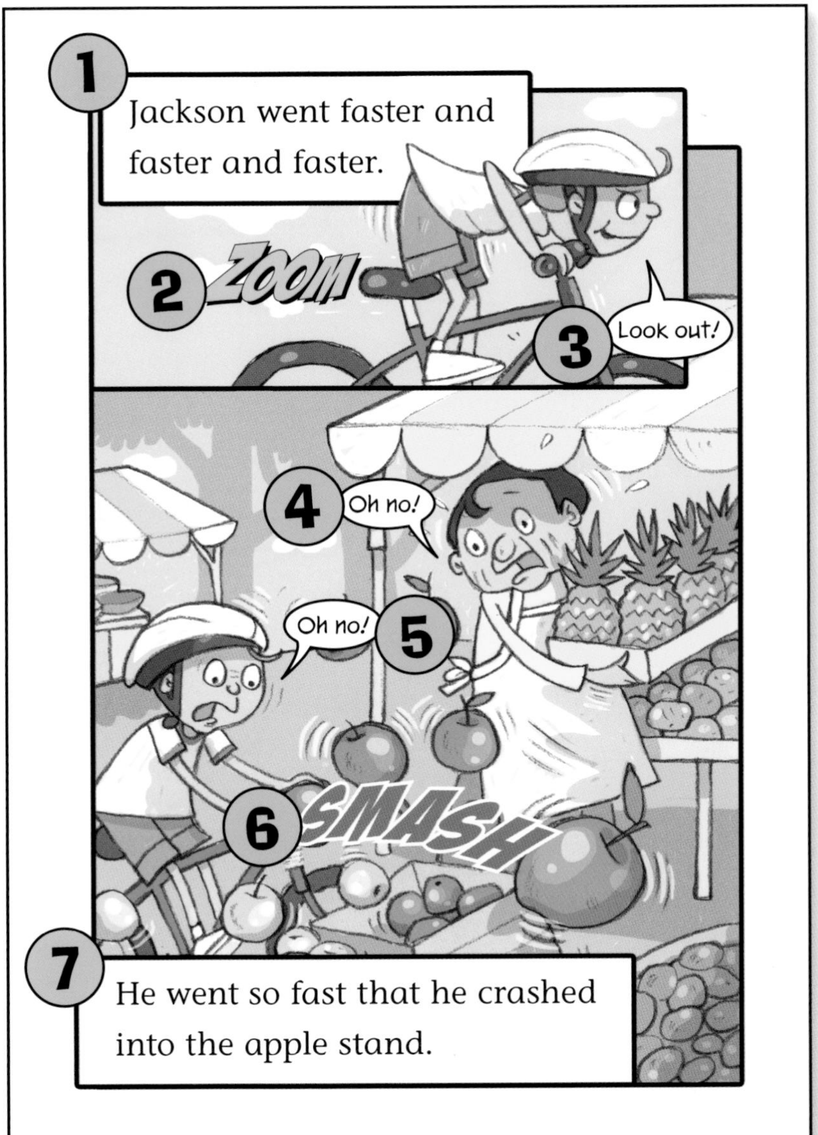
1
Jackson went faster and faster and faster.
2
ZOOM
3
Look out!
4
Oh no!
5
Oh no!
6
SMASH
7
He went so fast that he crashed into the apple stand.

The pictures and the words work together to tell the whole story.

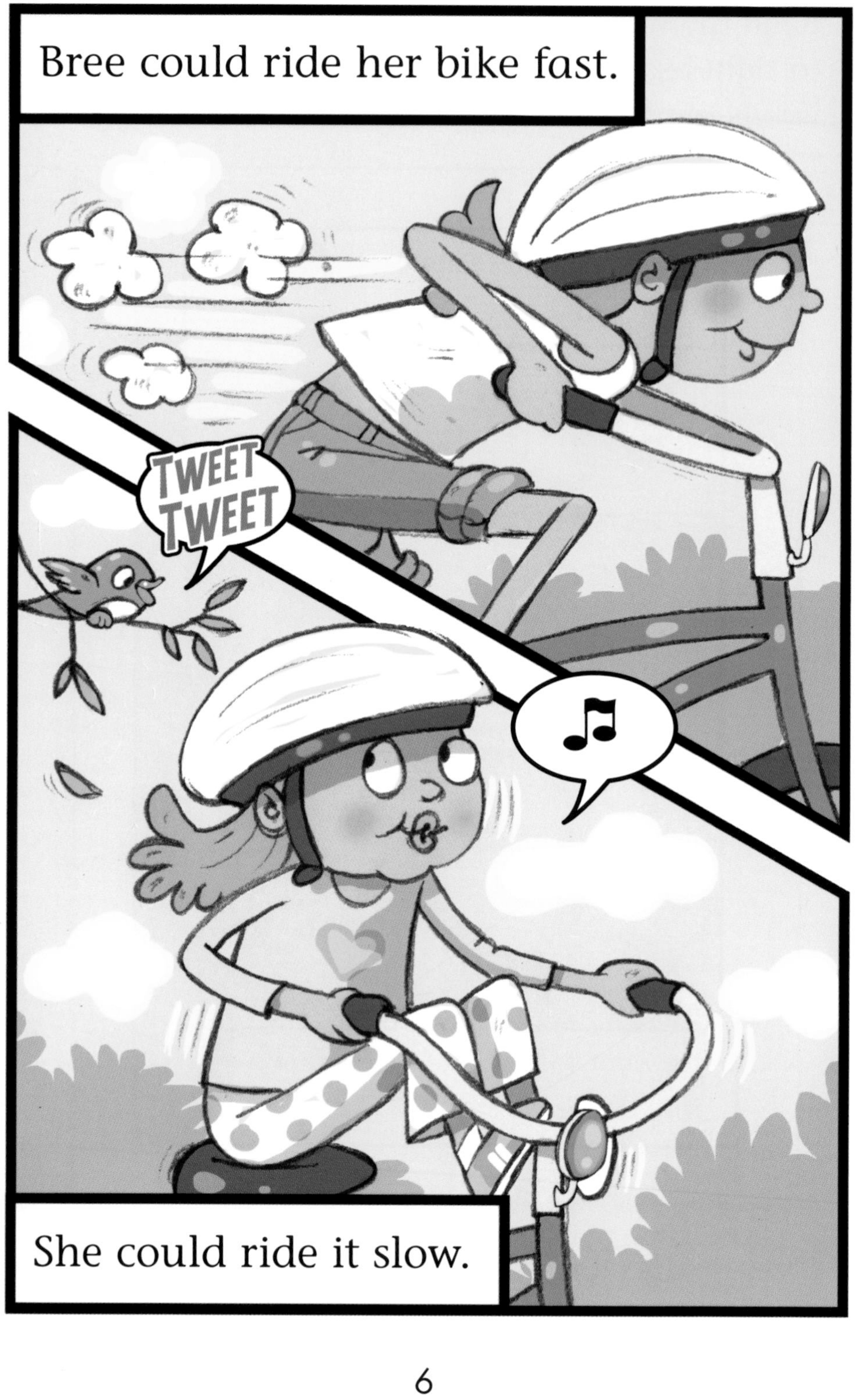
Bree could ride her bike fast.
TWEET TWEET
She could ride it slow.

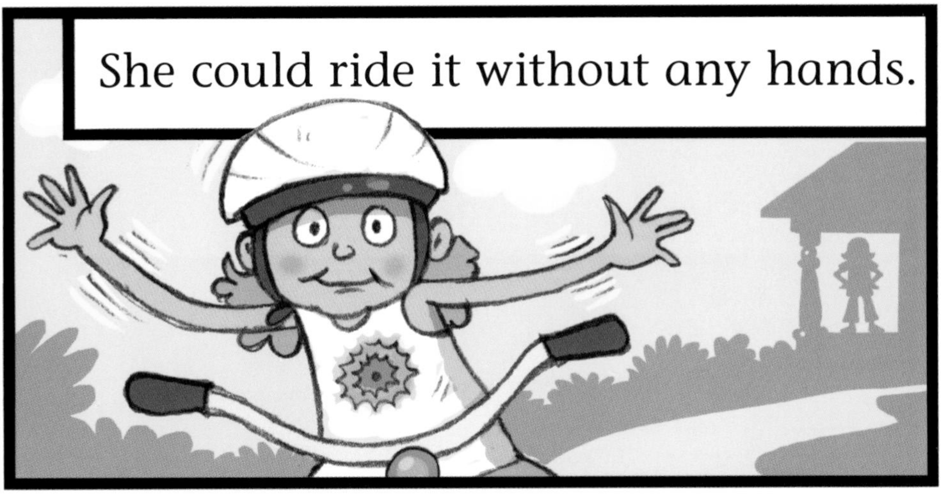
She could ride it without any hands.

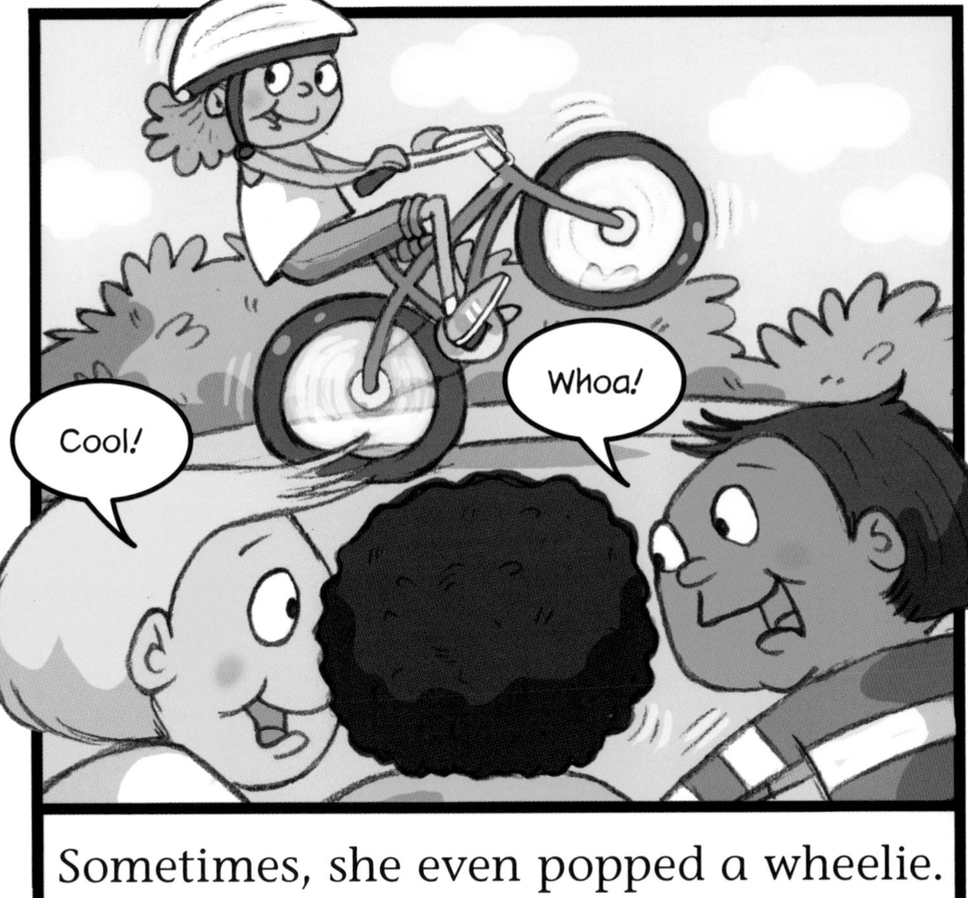
Whoa!
Cool!
Sometimes, she even popped a wheelie.

But Bree could not do the big jump in the field. It was too big. It was too steep. It was too scary.

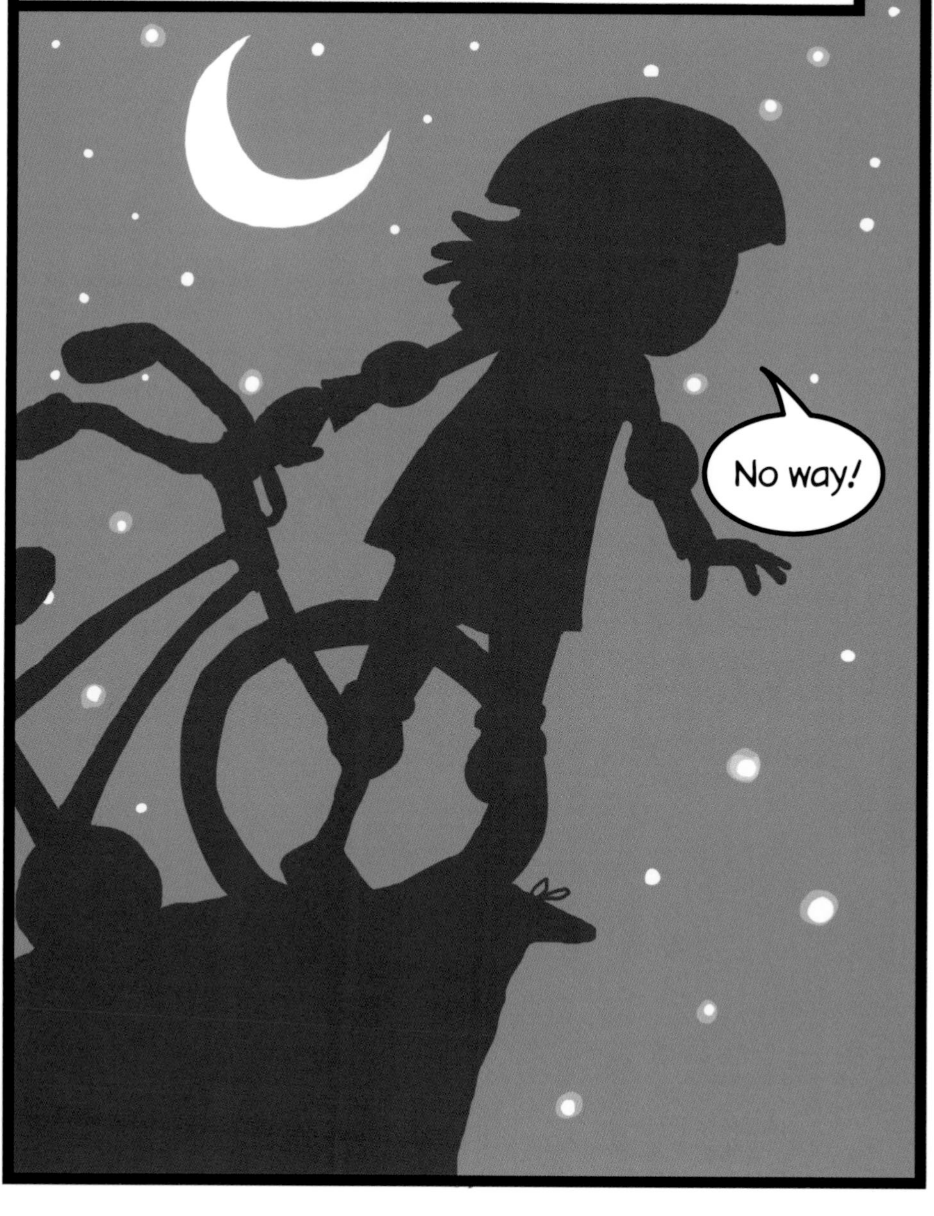
No way!

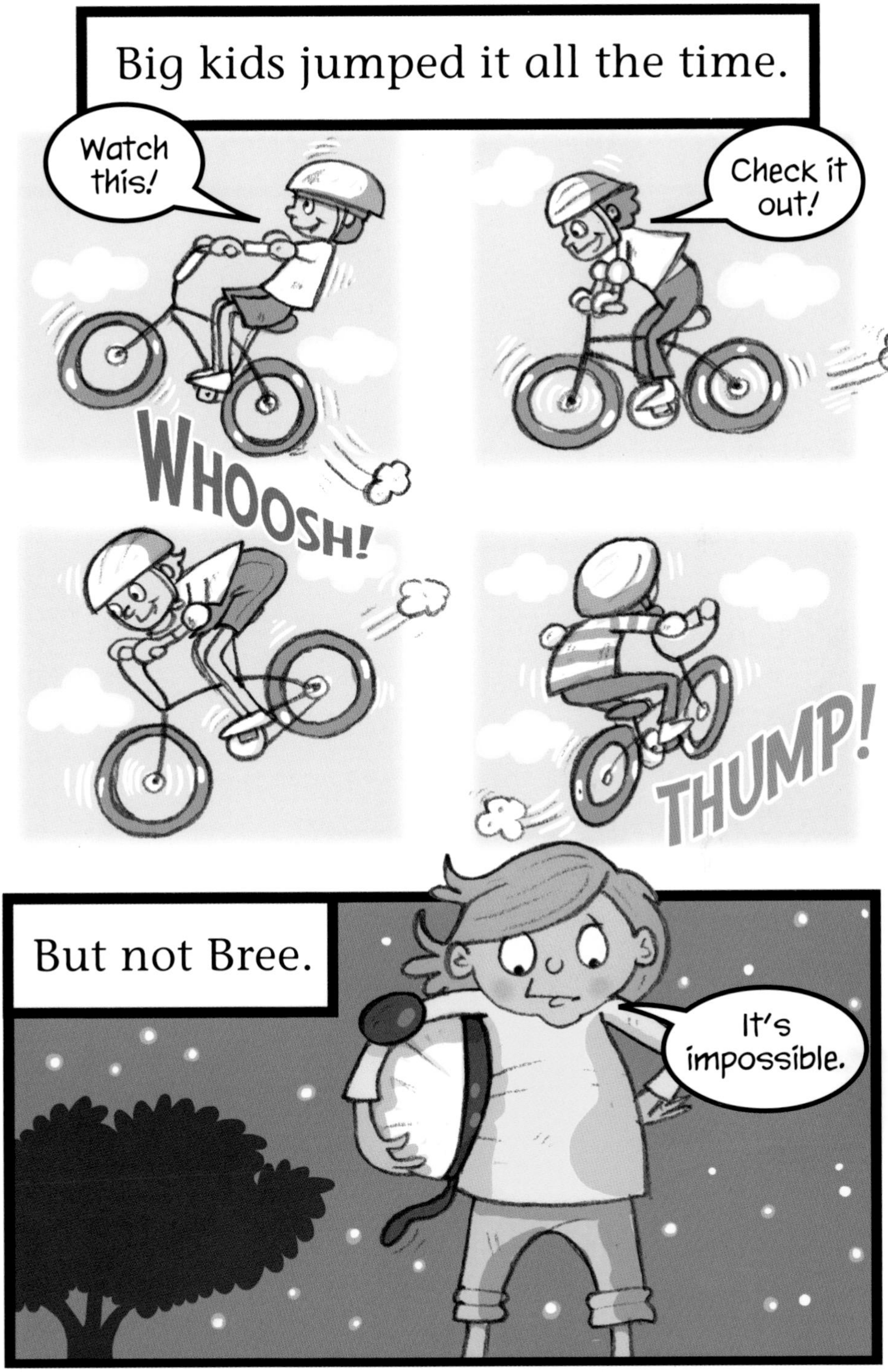
Big kids jumped it all the time.
Watch this!
Check it out!
WHOOSH!
THUMP!
But not Bree.
It's impossible.

Bree could only jump the small jump. It was not as steep. It was not as scary.

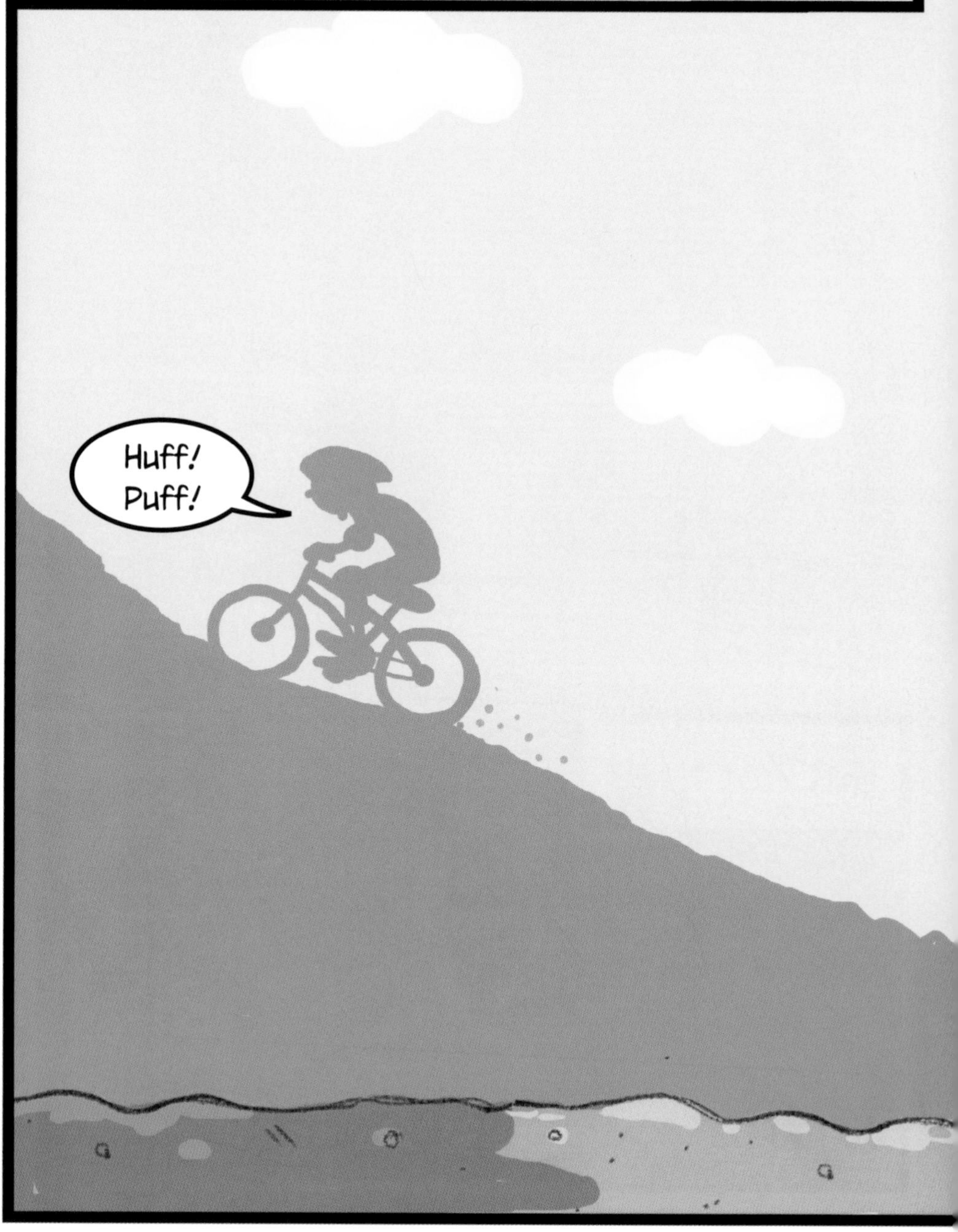
Huff!
Puff!

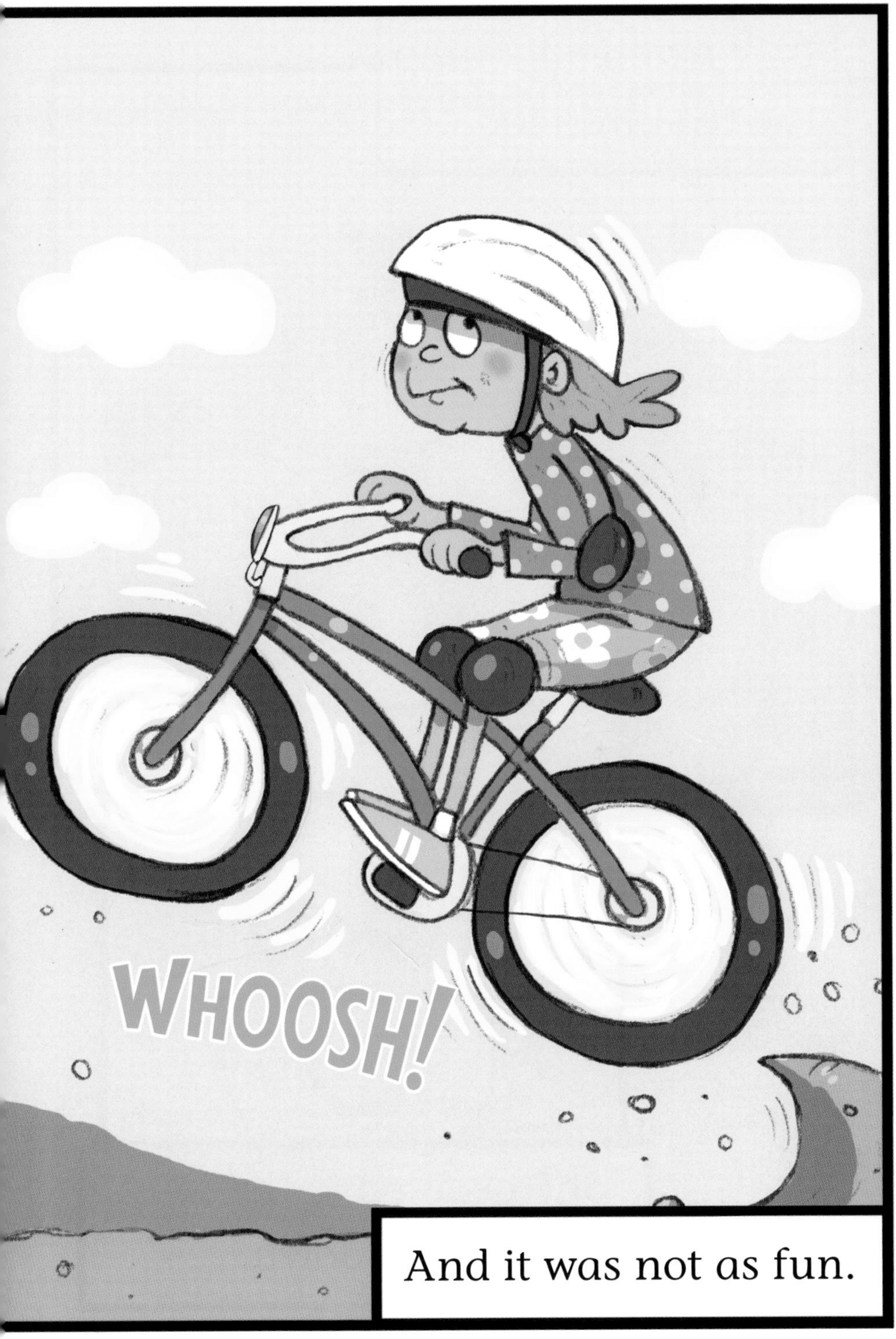
WHOOSH!

And it was not as fun.

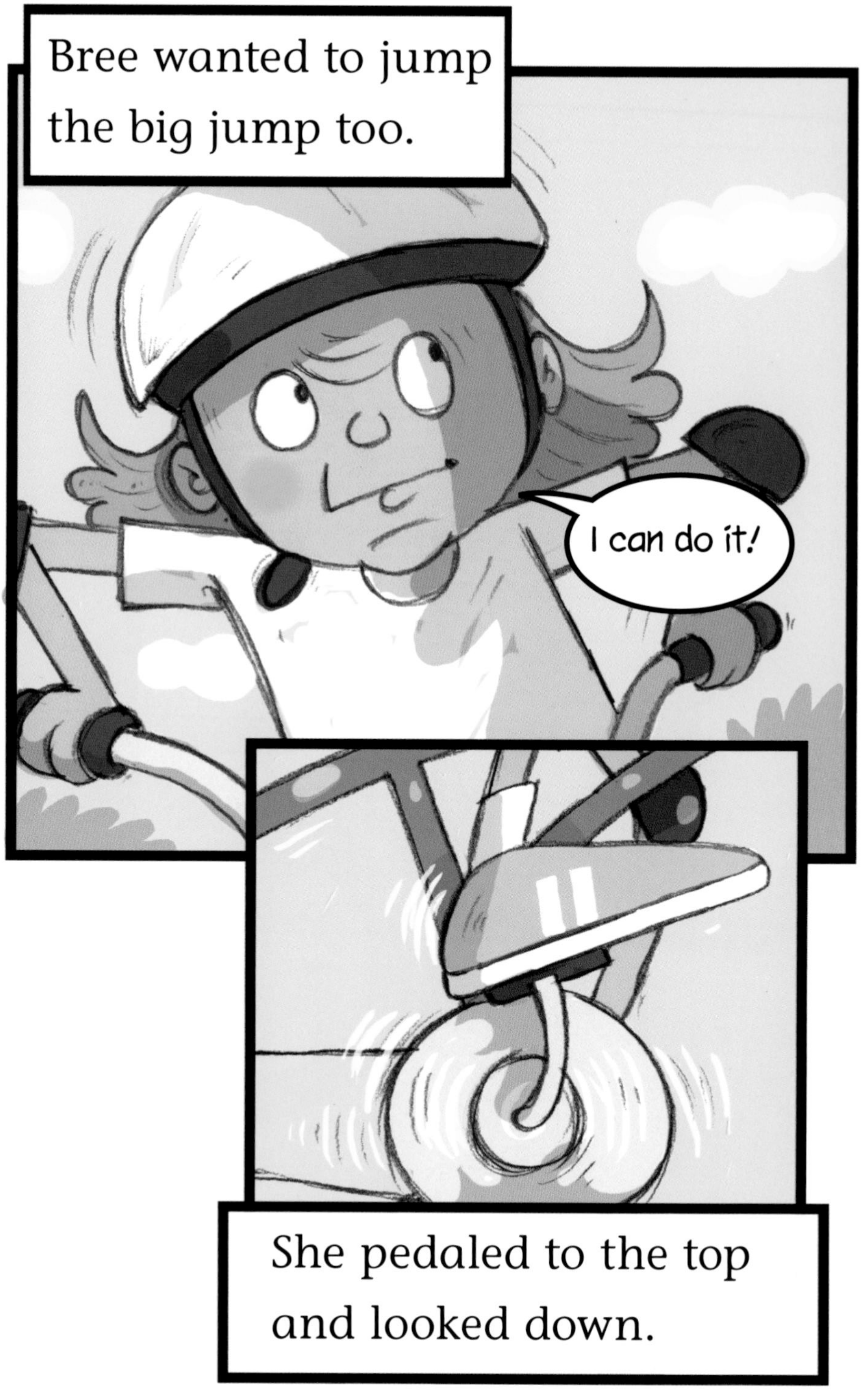
Bree wanted to jump the big jump too.
I can do it!
She pedaled to the top and looked down.

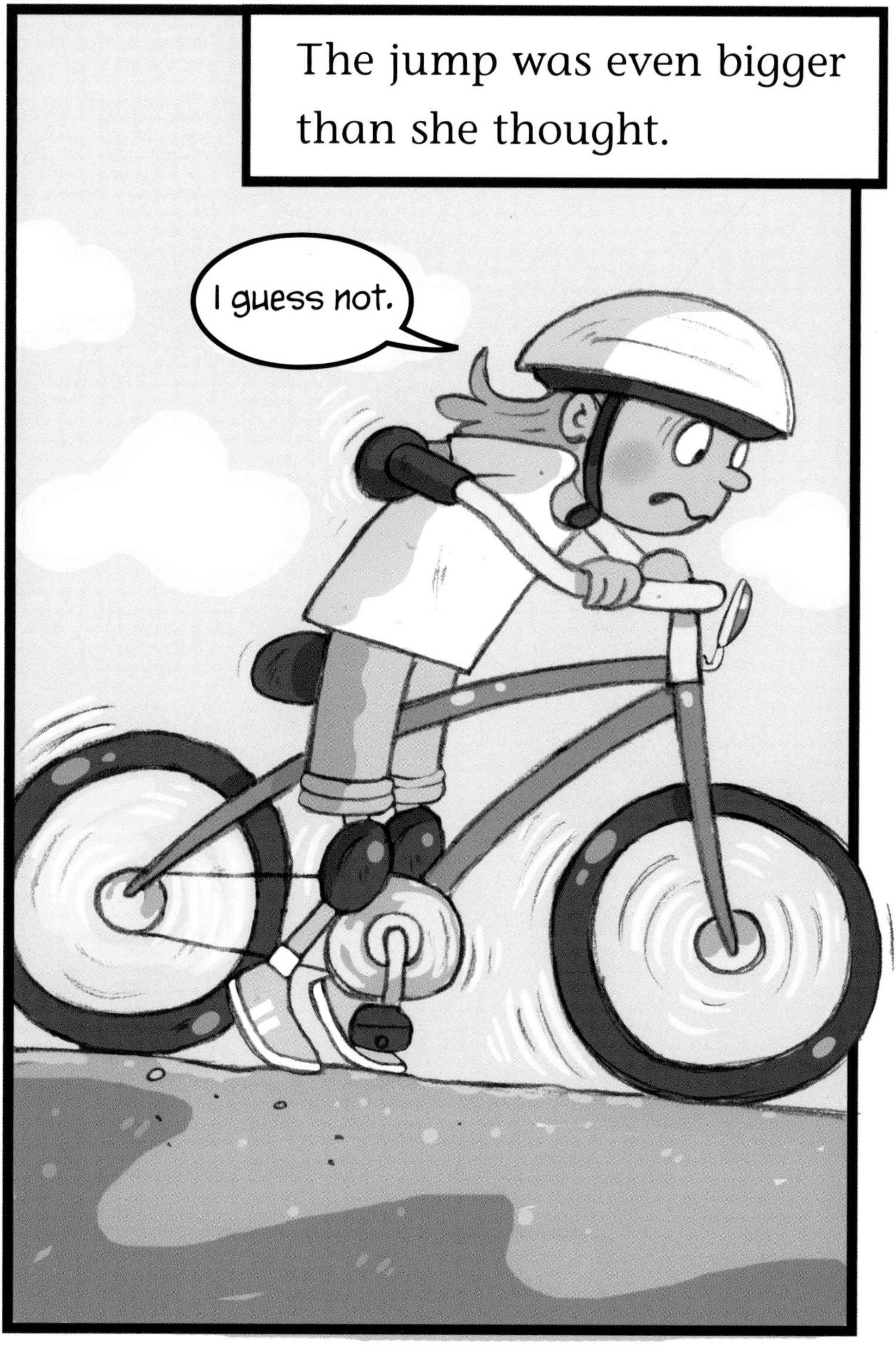
The jump was even bigger than she thought.
I guess not.

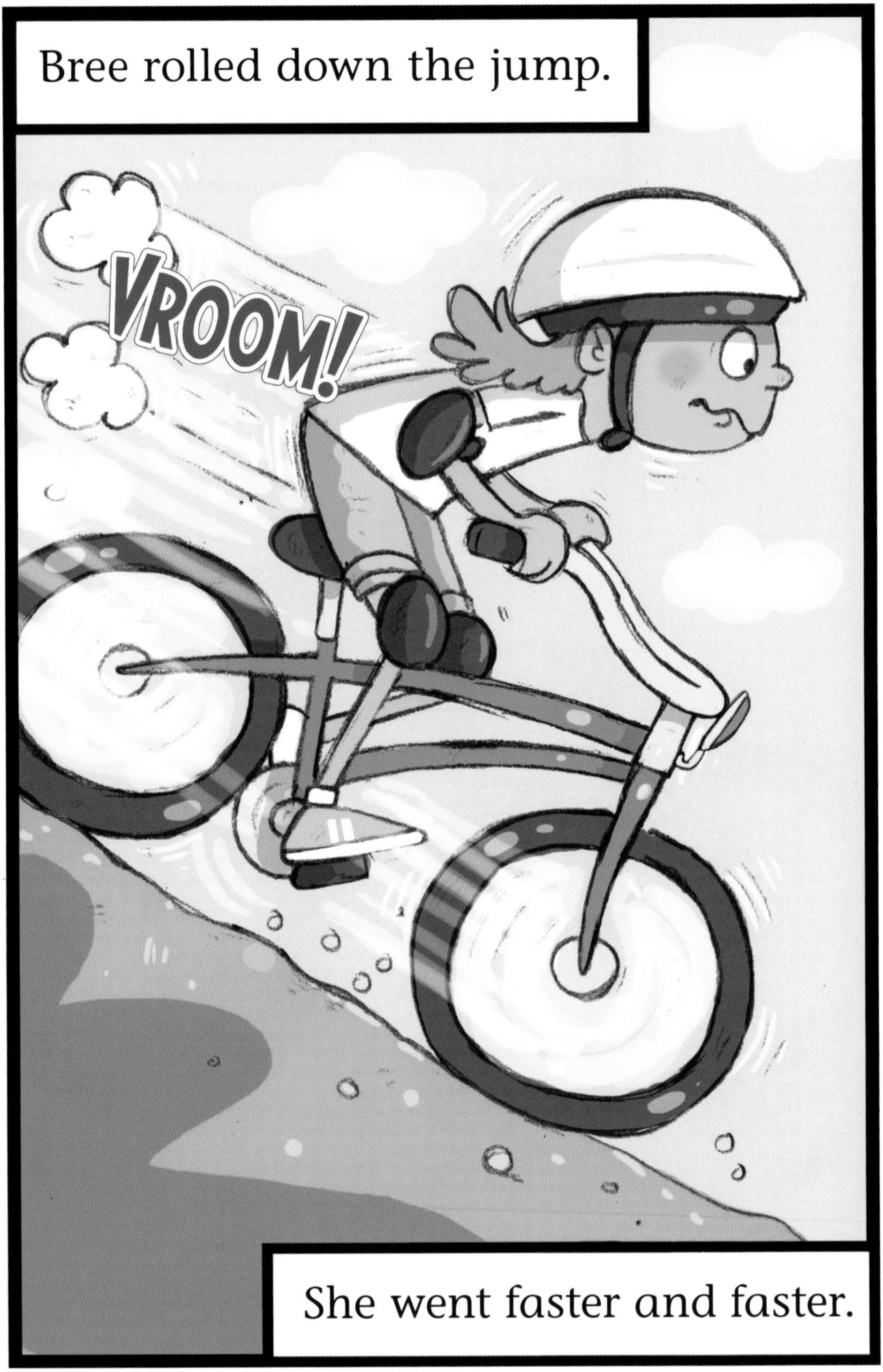
Bree rolled down the jump.
VROOM!
She went faster and faster.

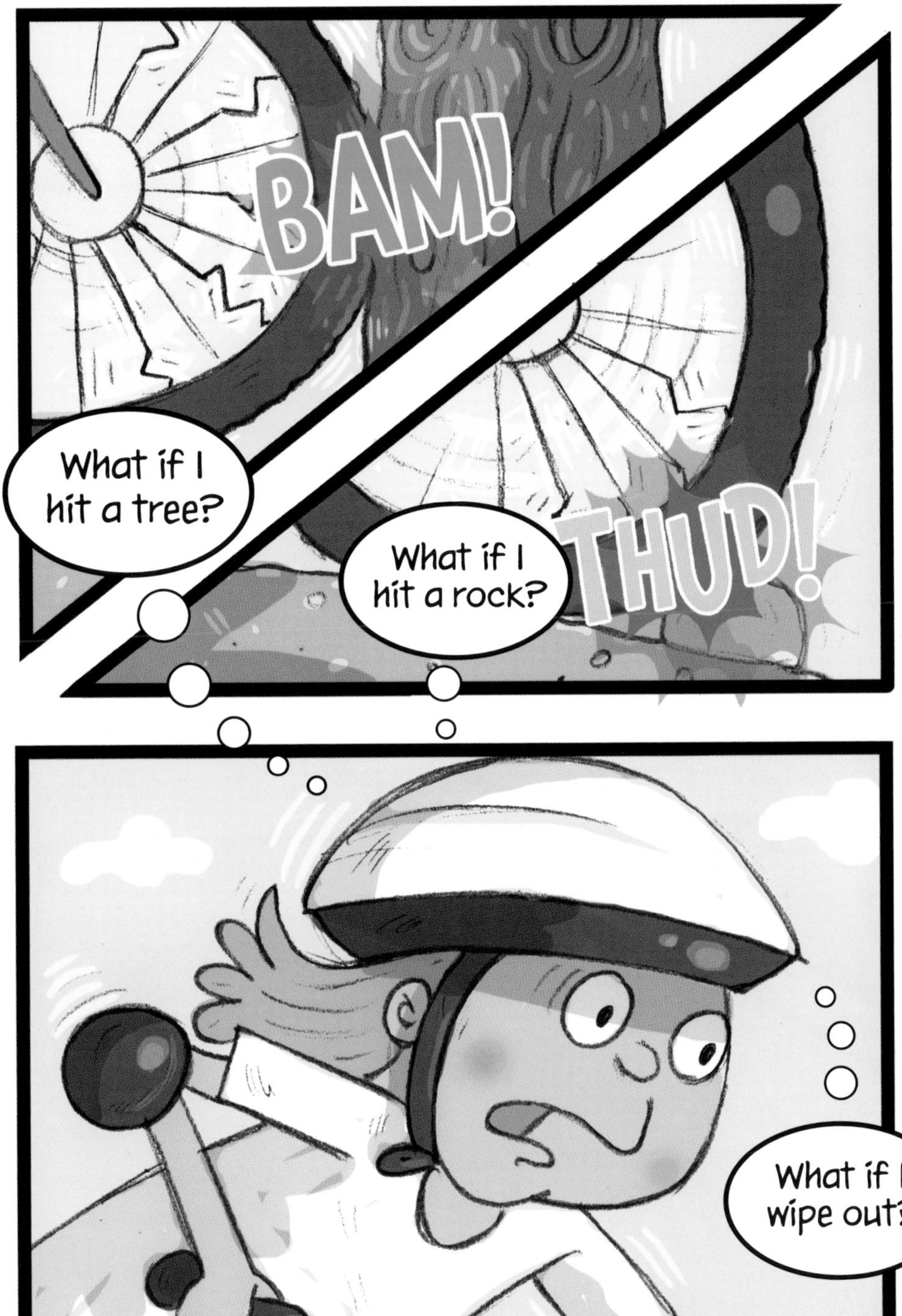
BAM!
What if I hit a tree?
What if I hit a rock?
THUD!
What if I wipe out?

At the last second, Bree slammed on her brakes.

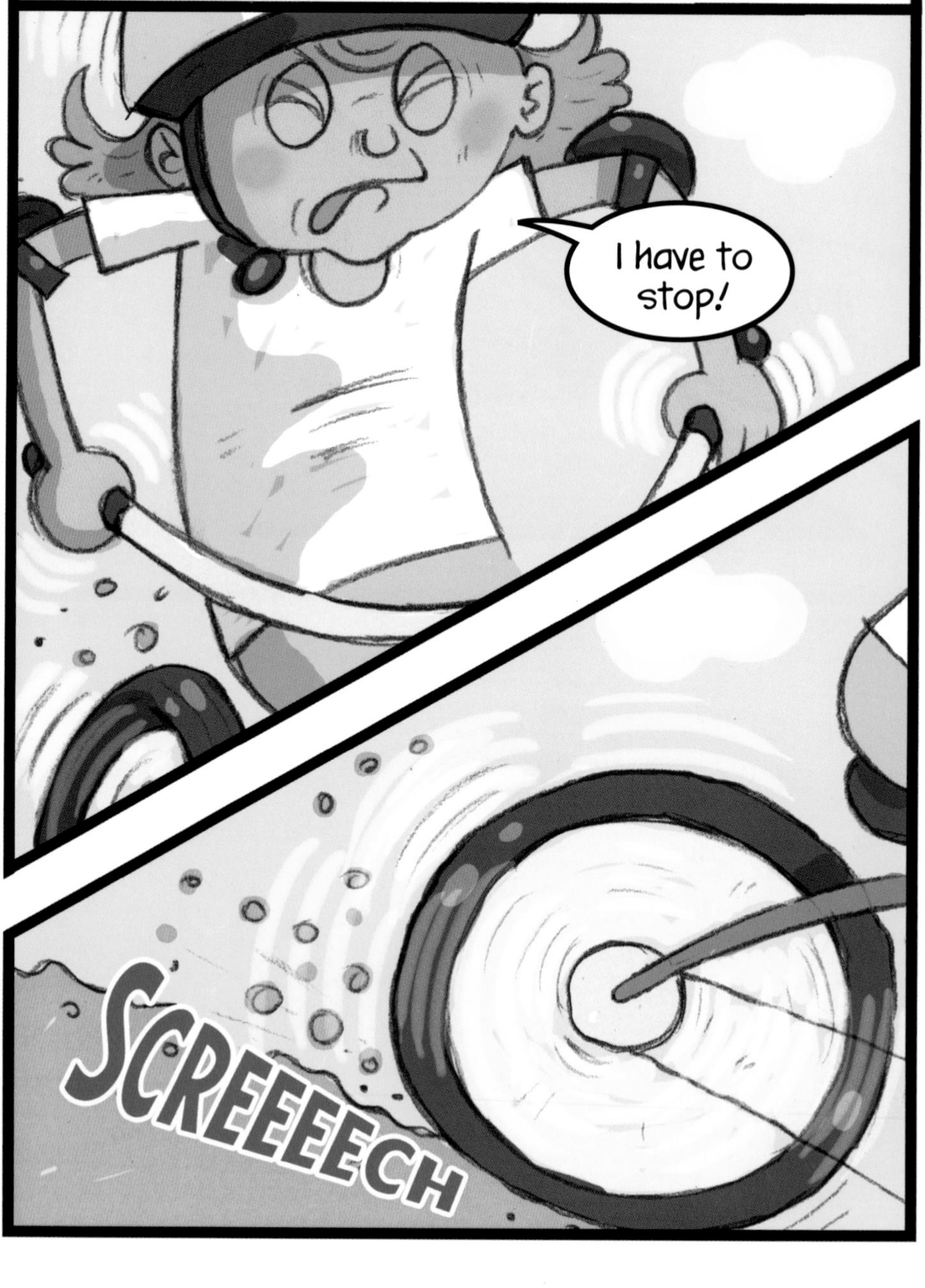
I have to stop!
SCREEEEECH

She could not do the big jump.
It was too big. It was too steep.
It was too scary.

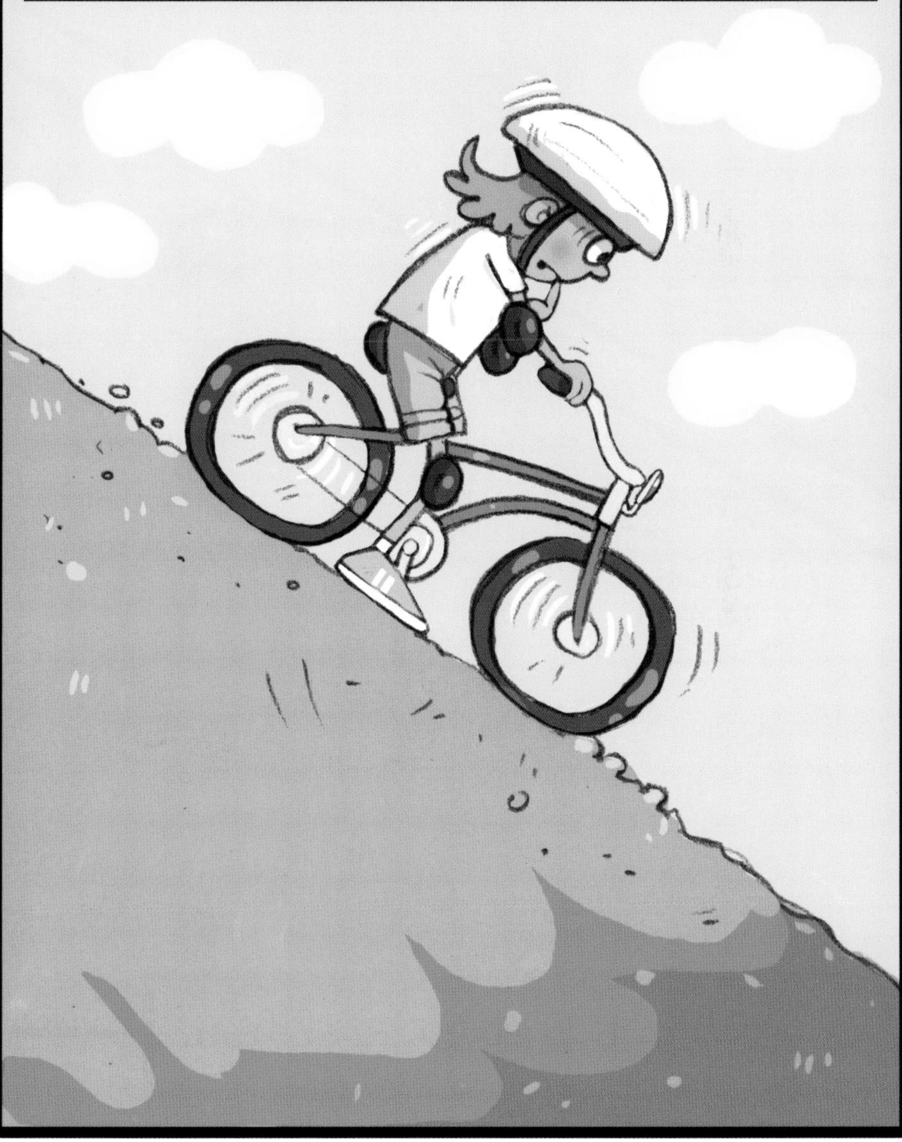

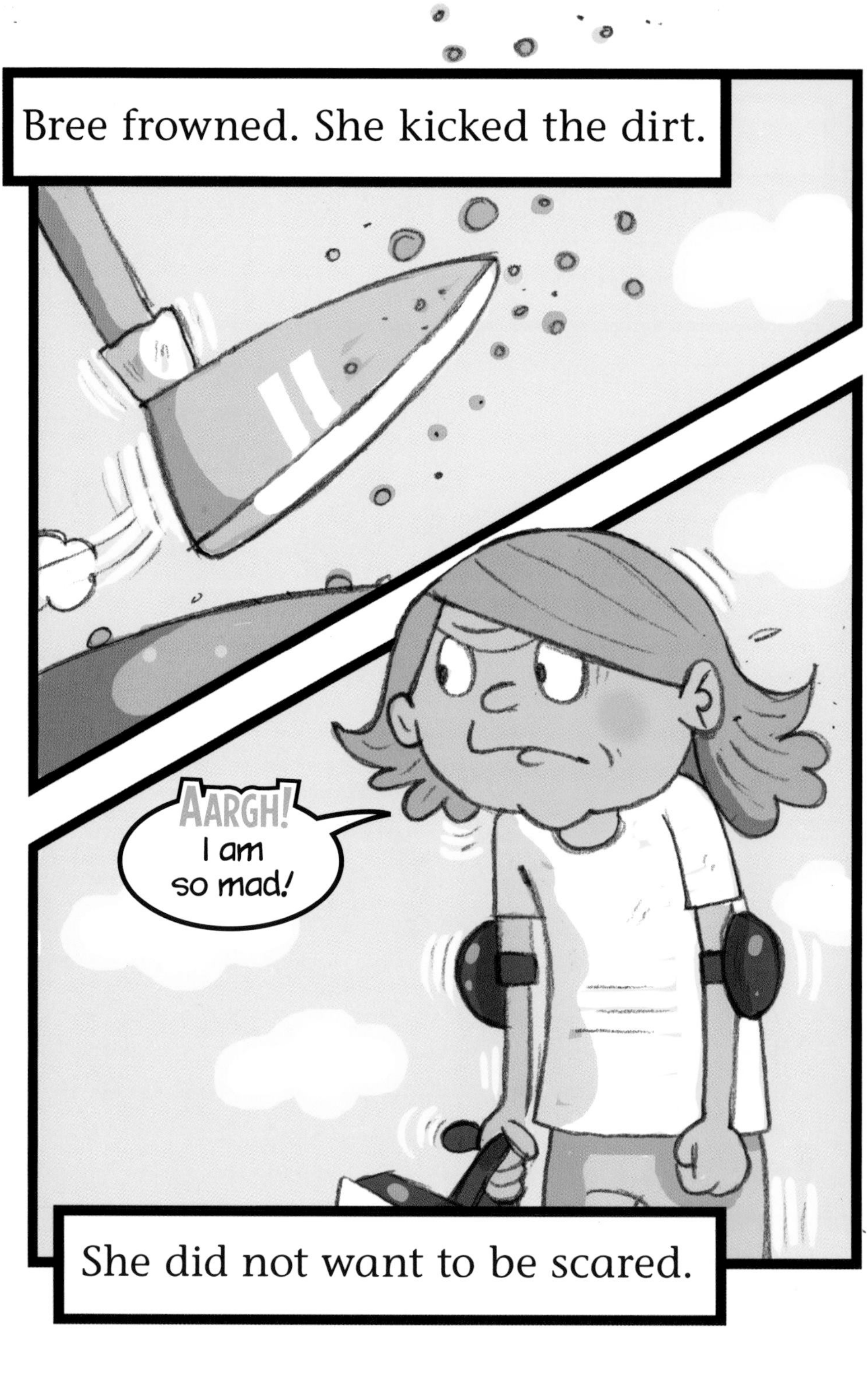
Bree frowned. She kicked the dirt.
AARGH! I am so mad!
She did not want to be scared.

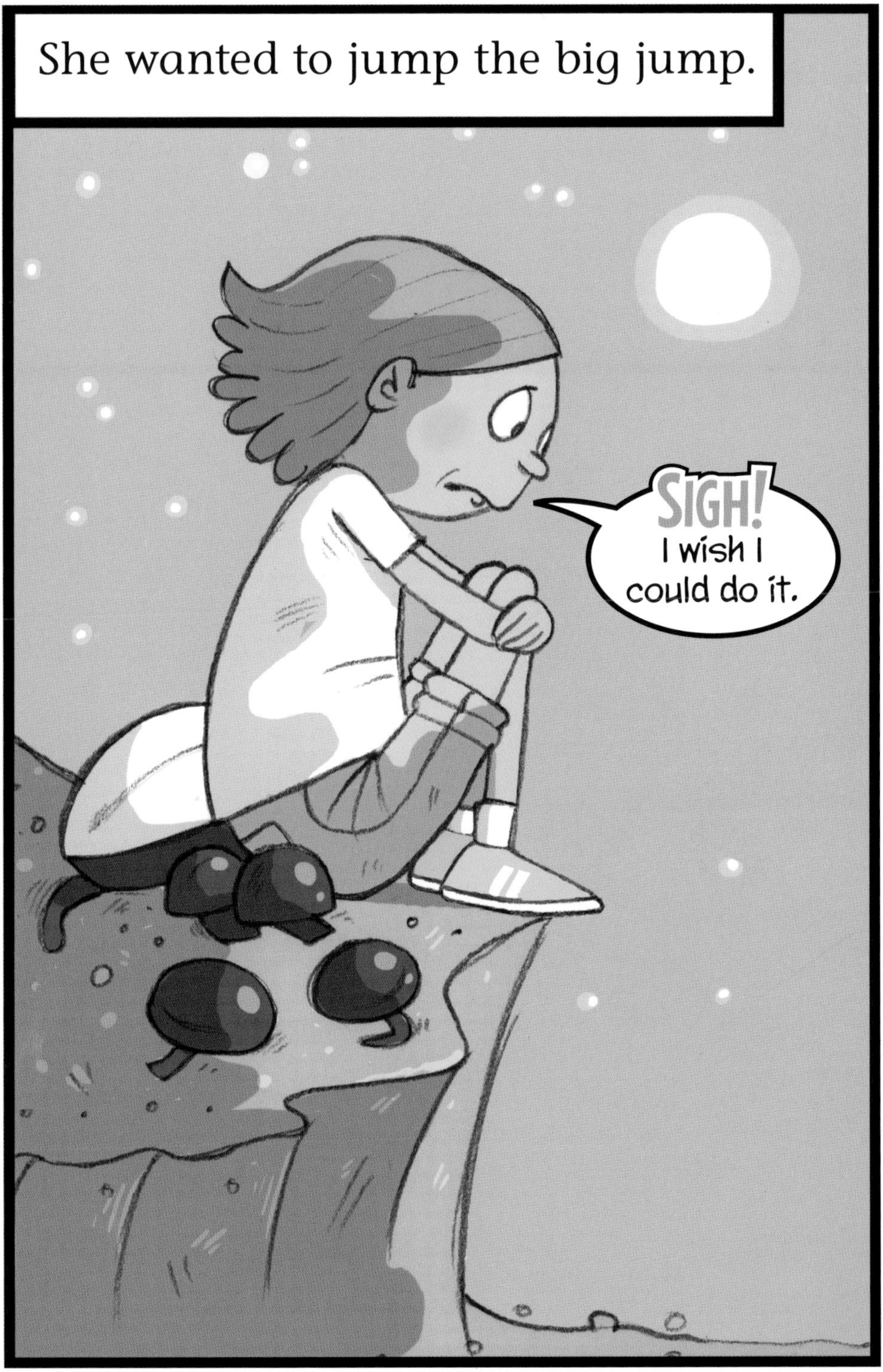
She wanted to jump the big jump.
SIGH! I wish I could do it.

Then Bree got an idea. She would make the small jump bigger. Each time she made it bigger, it would only be a little scarier.

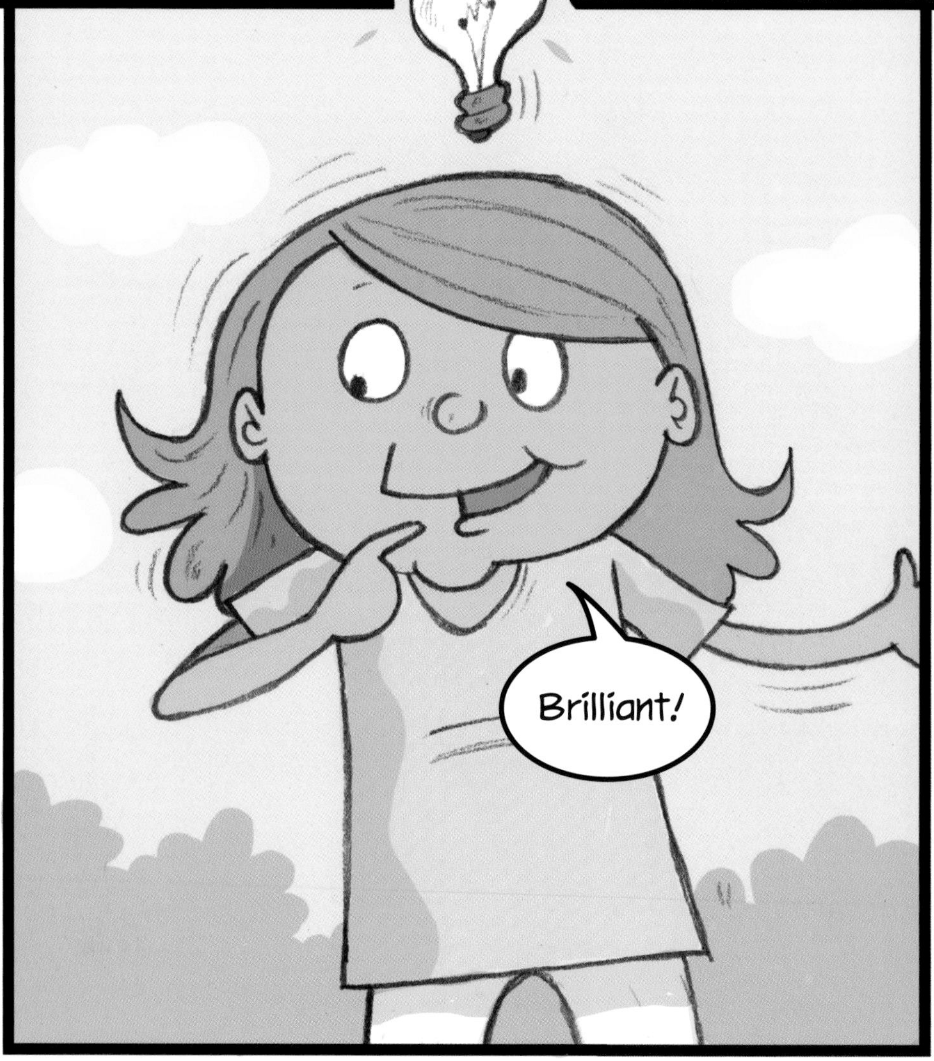
Brilliant!

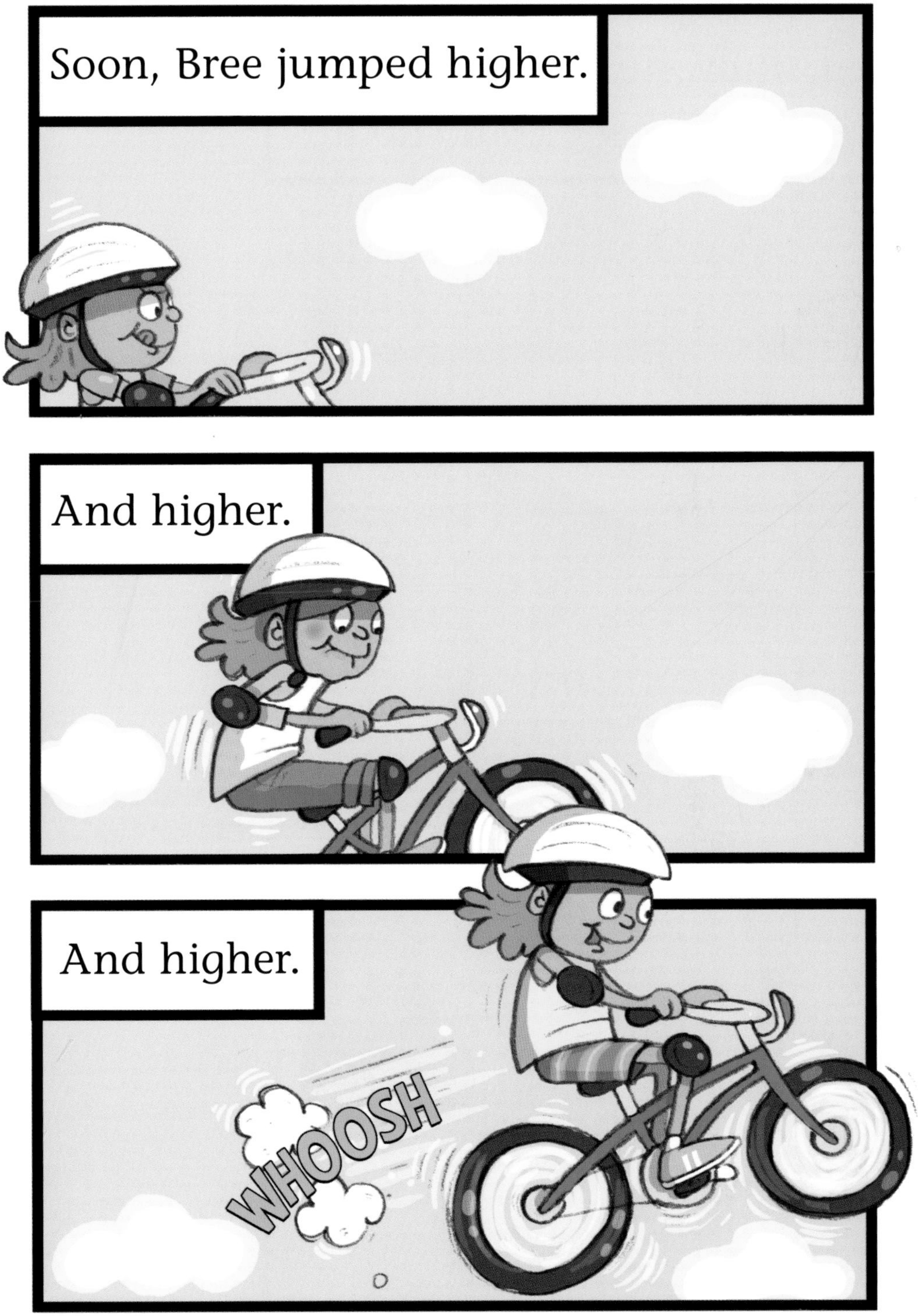
Soon, Bree jumped higher.
And higher.
And higher.
WHOOSH

Finally, Bree was ready.
She knew she could do it.

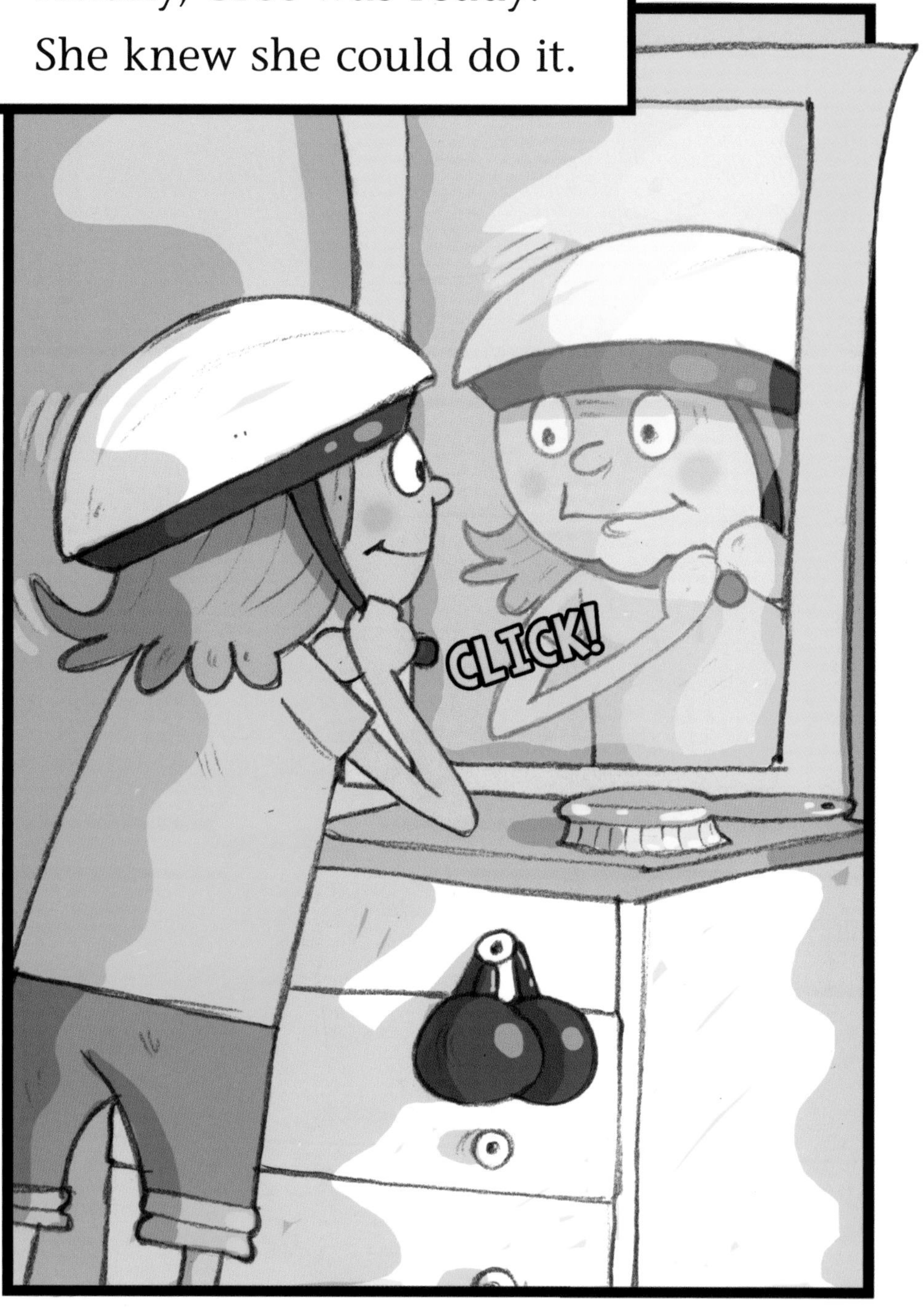
CLICK!

She raced to the top of the big jump and looked down. It was still big. It was still steep.

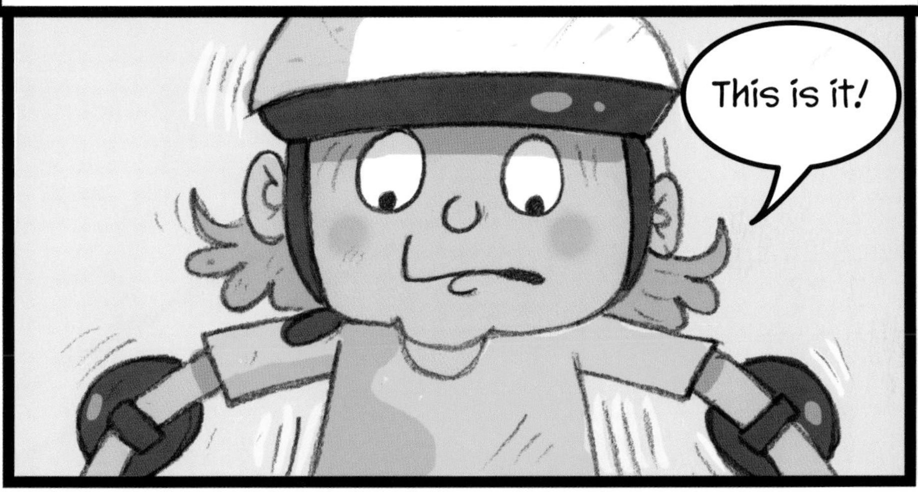
This is it!

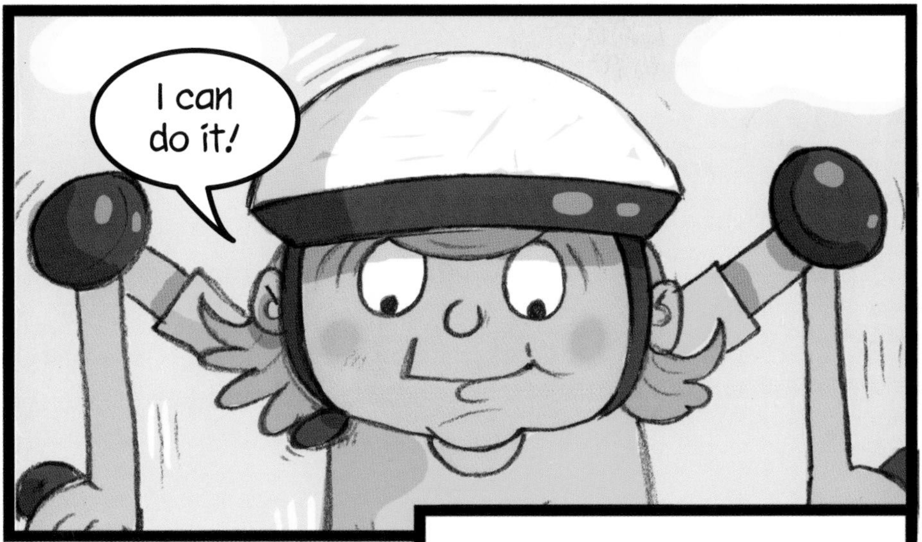
I can do it!

But it was not scary.

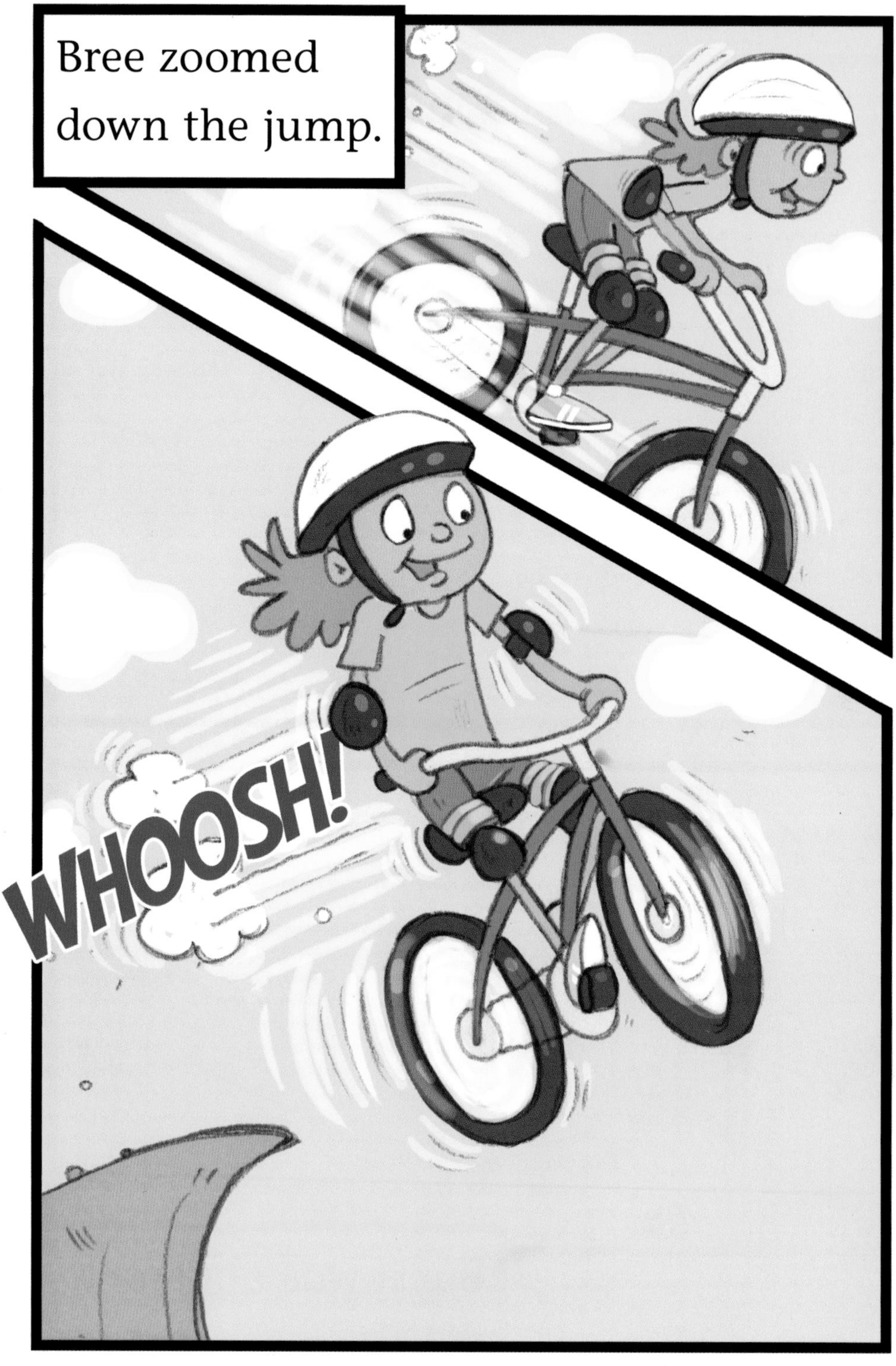
Bree zoomed down the jump.
WHOOSH!

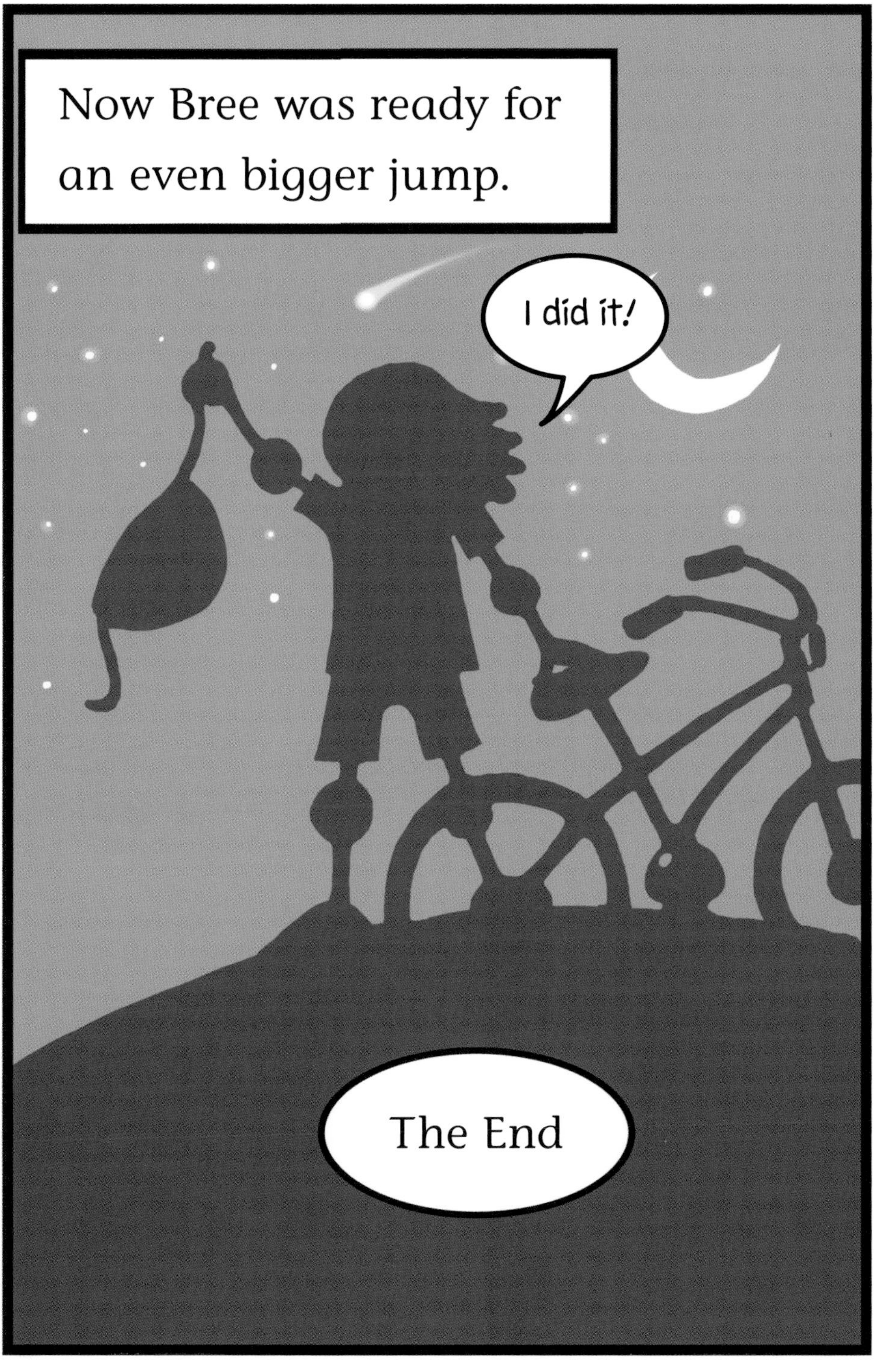
Now Bree was ready for an even bigger jump.
I did it!
The End

ABOUT THE AUTHOR

Lori Mortensen is a multi-published children's author who writes fiction and nonfiction on all sorts of subjects. When she's not plunking away at the keyboard, she enjoys making cheesy bread rolls, gardening, and hanging out with her family at their home in northern California.

ABOUT THE ILLUSTRATOR

Mary Sullivan has been drawing and writing her whole life, which has mostly been spent in Texas. She earned a BFA from the University of Texas in Studio Art but considers herself a self-trained illustrator. Mary lives in Cedar Park, a suburb of Austin, Texas. She loves to go swimming in the lake with her dog.

GLOSSARY

brakes (BRAYKS)—the things on your bike that help you slow down and stop

pedal (PED-uhl)—the items on your bike that you push in a circle with your foot

steep (STEEP)—sharply goes down

wheelie (WEE-lee)—to ride a bike with the front wheel off the ground

1.) When did you learn to ride a bike? Who helped you learn?

2.) Trying new things can be scary. Talk about a time when you tried something new.

3.) Would you try to jump the big jump? Why or why not?

WRITING PROMPTS

1.) Make up at least three new bike tricks. Write down the names of each one. Be sure to explain how to do each trick.

2.) If you could have any bike in the world, what would it look like? Draw a picture of your dream bike. Make sure to name it.

3.) Throughout the book, there are sound and action words next to some of the pictures. Pick at least two of those words. Then write your own sentences using those words.

MY 1ST GRAPHIC NOVEL

THE 1ST STEP INTO GRAPHIC NOVELS

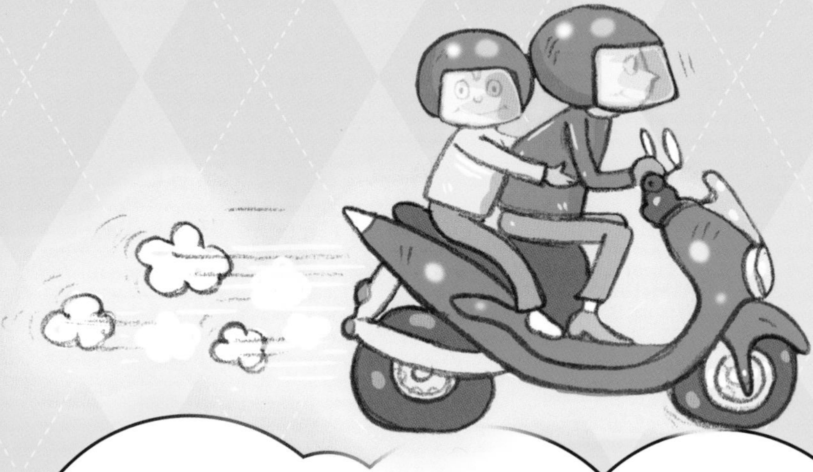

These books are the perfect introduction to graphic novels. Combine an entertaining story with comic book panels, exciting action elements, and bright colors, and a safe graphic novel is born.

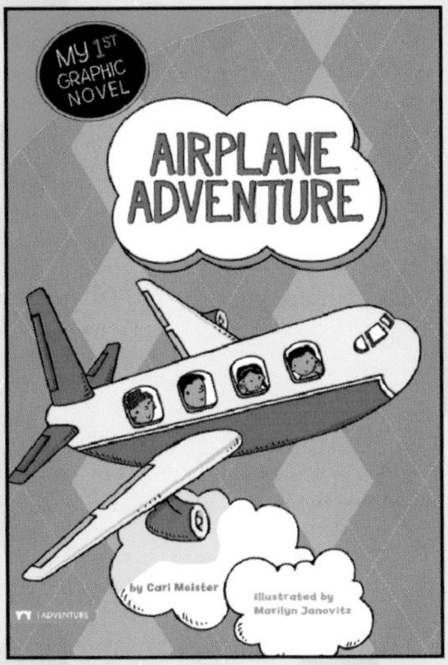
MY 1ST GRAPHIC NOVEL
AIRPLANE ADVENTURE
by Cari Meister
illustrated by Marilyn Janovitz
ADVENTURE

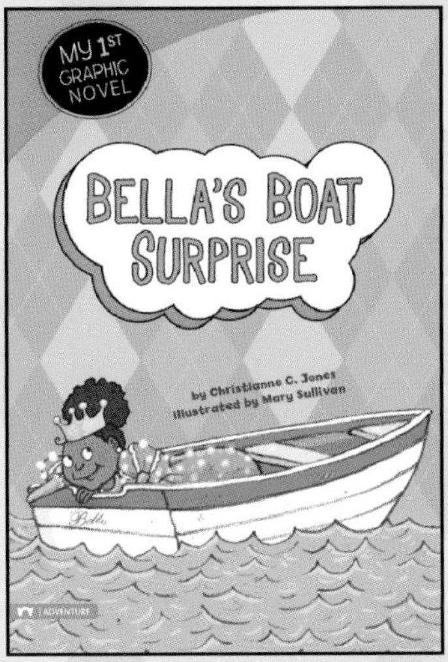
MY 1ST GRAPHIC NOVEL
BELLA'S BOAT SURPRISE
by Christianne C. Jones
illustrated by Mary Sullivan
Bella
ADVENTURE

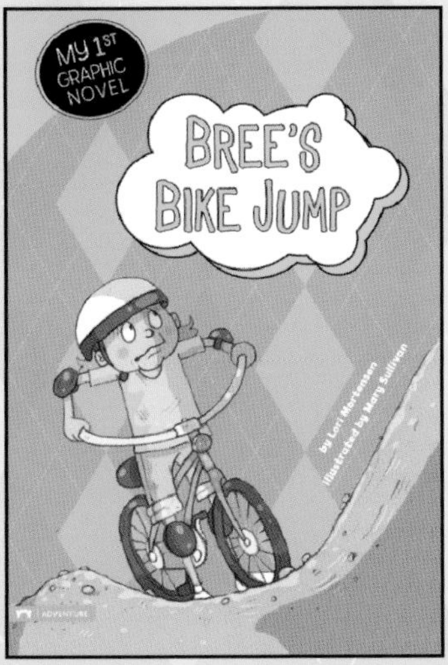
MY 1ST GRAPHIC NOVEL
BREE'S BIKE JUMP
by Lori Mortensen
illustrated by Mary Sullivan
ADVENTURE

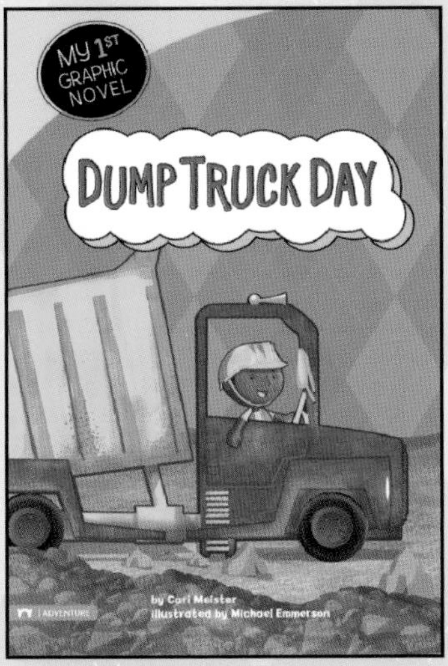
MY 1ST GRAPHIC NOVEL
DUMP TRUCK DAY
by Cari Meister
illustrated by Michael Emmerson
ADVENTURE

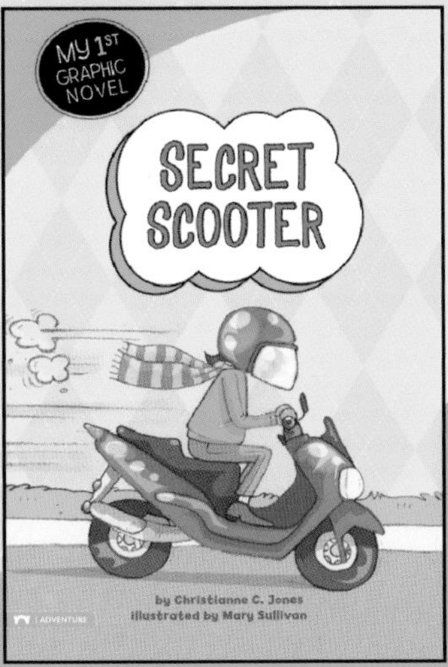
MY 1ST GRAPHIC NOVEL
SECRET SCOOTER
by Christianne C. Jones
illustrated by Mary Sullivan
ADVENTURE

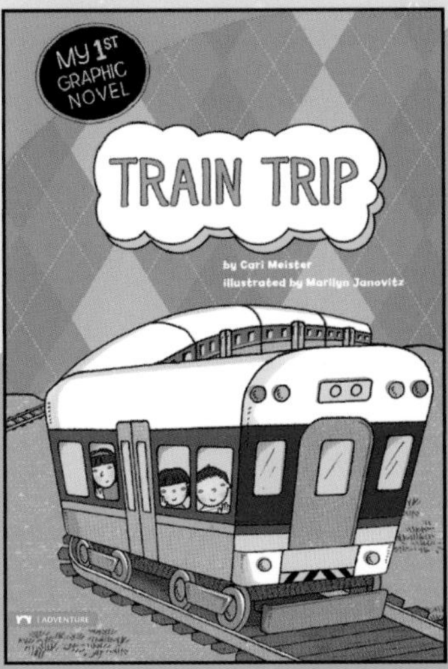
MY 1ST GRAPHIC NOVEL
TRAIN TRIP
by Cari Meister
illustrated by Marilyn Janovitz
ADVENTURE